Hello, Family Members,

Learning to read is one of the most important accomplishments of early childhood. **Hello Reader!** books are designed to help children become skilled readers who like to read. Beginning readers learn to read by remembering frequently used words like "the," "is," and "and"; by using phonics skills to decode new words; and by interpreting picture and text clues. These books provide both the stories children enjoy and the structure they need to read fluently and independently. Here are suggestions for helping your child *before*, *during*, and *after* reading:

Before
- Look at the cover and pictures and have your child predict what the story is about.
- Read the story to your child.
- Encourage your child to chime in with familiar words and phrases.
- Echo read with your child by reading a line first and having your child read it after you do.

During
- Have your child think about a word he or she does not recognize right away. Provide hints such as "Let's see if we know the sounds" and "Have we read other words like this one?"
- Encourage your child to use phonics skills to sound out new words.
- Provide the word for your child when more assistance is needed so that he or she does not struggle and the experience of reading with you is a positive one.
- Encourage your child to have fun by reading with a lot of expression . . . like an actor!

After
- Have your child keep lists of interesting and favorite words.
- Encourage your child to read the books over and over again. Have him or her read to brothers, sisters, grandparents, and even teddy bears. Repeated readings develop confidence in young readers.
- Talk about the stories. Ask and answer questions. Share ideas about the funniest and most interesting characters and events in the stories.

I do hope that you and your child enjoy this book.

—Francie Alexander
Reading Specialist,
Scholastic's Learning Ventures

For Rebecca
—G.H.

For Julianna,
who's an artist too
—P.B.F.

Text copyright © 1999 by Gail Herman.
Illustrations copyright © 1999 by Paige Billin-Frye.
All rights reserved. Published by Scholastic Inc.
SCHOLASTIC, HELLO READER and CARTWHEEL BOOKS and associated logos
are trademarks and/or registered trademarks of Scholastic Inc.

Library of Congress Cataloging-in-Publication Data
Herman, Gail.
    Slip! slide! skate! / by Gail Herman; illustrated by Paige Billin-Frye.
    p. cm. — (Hello reader! Level 2)
"Cartwheel books."
Summary: a young girl who wants to be the best ice skater in the whole class
learns that it is just as important to have fun.
    ISBN 0-439-09907-2
    [1. Ice skating Fiction. 2. Perfectionism (Personality trait) Fiction.]
I. Billin-Frye, Paige, ill. II. Title. III. Series.
PZ7.H4315S 1999
[E]—DC21
                                                    99-31526
                                                       CIP
                                                        AC
10 9 8 7 6 5   0/0 01 02 03 04
                        Printed in the U.S.A.   24
                        First printing, December 1999

Slip! Slide! Skate!

by Gail Herman
Illustrated by Paige Billin-Frye

Hello Reader!— Level 2

SCHOLASTIC INC.

New York   Toronto   London   Auckland   Sydney   Mexico City   New Delhi   Hong Kong

"I have a surprise for you,"
Mom tells me.
"Ice skates!"
My first pair!
Soon I will be the best
ice-skater on my block.

Mom takes me for lessons.
Annie, the teacher, shows us
how to lace our skates.
Easy! I think.

Then we all stand up.
My feet feel wobbly.

Oops! I sit down.
"Do you need help?"
asks Annie.

"No thanks," I answer.

"I need help!" says Beth.

Annie takes us onto the ice.
I stumble a bit.
But we all hold the railing.

"Now let go!" Annie calls.

"And glide if you can!"

"Of course I can,"

I whisper.

"I'm going to be the best!"

I move slowly.
But I am doing it.
I am gliding!

"Ow!"
Beth falls down next to me.
Annie and I help her up.
Beth giggles
and falls down again.
"This is fun," she says.

Falling down is fun?
I shake my head.
Beth will never be the best.

Weeks go by,
and now I skate
even better.

I slide and glide
and zoom and zip

I am the best skater
in our whole class!

"Next week we will be in
the Ice Show,"
Annie tells us.
"You will skate in a line,
holding hands."

That is too easy, I think.
Beth laughs and claps her hands.
"That sounds like fun!" she says.
I look at her and frown.
"We are not here to have fun,"
I say.
"We are here to put on a show!"

We practice holding hands
and skating.
I am getting bored.
I want to slide and glide
and zoom and zip.
So everyone knows
I am the best!

Then it is the day of the Ice Show.
I watch the other skaters.
They are so pretty.
They move like ballerinas.

Now it is our turn.
I am in the lead.
I hold Beth's hand.
Beth holds Lisa's hand.
Lisa holds Jack's hand.
Jack holds Ben's hand.
We glide in a straight line.
I know we look nice.
But those other skaters?
They are the best.
Unless . . .

We go faster!
I speed up.
Beth speeds up.

So do Lisa and Jack
and Ben.
Now we are moving!

I do not notice a bump in the ice.
I trip over the bump,
and fall—*splat*—on the ground.
I pull down Beth.
Beth pulls down Lisa.
Lisa pulls down Jack.
And Jack pulls down Ben.

Oh, no!
I have ruined the show!

Then Beth laughs.
Lisa and Jack and Ben laugh, too.
Everyone is laughing.
All at once, I giggle.
I try to stand up.
But I fall down again.
Now I laugh harder.

I am not the best,
I think.
But this is a lot more fun!